Radha & The Rainbow Cycle

by

Ruchi lal

First Published in 2023

Becomeshakespeare.com

One Point Six Technologies Pvt Ltd
123, Building J2, Shram Seva Premises,
Wadala Truck Depot,
Wadala (East), Mumbai 400037, India
T: +91 8080226699

ISBN - 978-93-5667-451-6

Dedicated To

My Grandfather Late Shri Awadh Kumar Lal

&

To my daughters Yuvakshi & Aadya

Acknowledgement

To the relationships I have been blessed with, this is a small way of saying 'Thank You'!

I have dedicated this book primarily to my Dadaji, late Shri Awadh Kumar Lal, from whom I inherited a love for literature and his ability to pen his thoughts. He introduced me to the world of Maugham, Dickens, and the Bronte Sisters and made me understand the difference between literature and general reading.

My parents, who guided me towards the right kind of books; the ones that inspired me to be a writer in the first place. They were the ones who knew that I could be whoever I wanted to be, and I could do whatever I wanted to do.

My second set of parents, my in-laws, who have stood by me through everything and provided all the support I have needed in my career.

Mrs Sharmila Kantha, who has been my mentor and inspiration since day 1. Thank you for always showing immense confidence in me.

I must thank my husband too, who has been my moral compass, my sounding board, my best friend and foremost critique.

My children who have contributed immensely to this book and listened to my stories and their "mummy tell us more" which inspired more and more chapters.

My brother, without whom none of my achievements throughout my life would have been possible.

My friends, who read the first draft and pointed out the flaws.

Ayushi, my illustrator & Becoming Shakespeare, who helped me throughout this journey.

Thank you all for making me better bit by bit.

I would also like to dedicate this to my daughters Yuvakshi & Aadya

Contents

Chapter 1

A New Beginning

A wide spread of green valleys and hillocks, on which you could see a goat grazing here and there. A meandering brook which made the most wonderful gurgling sounds. And *amidst* all of these, in a moving car you could see a pair of the brown, sparkling eyes peeping out of the rolled down window enjoying the cool wind blowing on her face and the smell of nature all around her. Nestled in the lap of the valley was a small township called Kamalapur in the state of Bihar, named after the Kamala River. One of its tributaries flowed right through the little hamlet.

Soon they reached a huge officers' bungalow, a low roofed expanse of brick & mortar which seemed to have seen so many stories, surrounded by a widespread lawn embroidered with flowers of all sorts of colours and a guava tree which was home to a pair of lively parrots. The car rolled over the pebbled driveway and came to a halt. Everyone hurriedly tumbled out of the car to inspect the property. The people who stepped out of the car were the new magistrate Mr. Narain, his wife Mrs. Narain, his ageing mother, and in the end slid out a little 10-year-old girl Radha who could not contain her excitement at moving to a new town and a new house.

The entire family went inside the house and were greeted by the bungalow's *maali kaka*, Bahadur the guard, and Savita Didi. Little Miss Radha had her eyes glued to a lock on the door of a garage situated in the east corner of the compound. Her mind was already full of images and ideas of things that might have been stacked there. Items that could tell stories of the past family, who probably had a little girl too. But since it was already evening and the Sun was yawning, all ready to go to bed, the Narains decided to unpack the next day. Everyone went inside the bungalow ready for their new lives to start.

The next morning, Radha woke up to a lot of banter throughout the house. Everyone was extremely busy: some cleaning, some unpacking. Maali kaka was running around the house with boxes and Savita Didi was busy dusting the whole place. *Amma* (Mrs Narain), was arranging everything in their rooms and

Baba (Mr Narain) was overseeing everything. *Dadi* was also busy arranging her *pooja* and helping *Amma*. Even though she was quite old, Dadi had a lot of energy and zeal, something she and Radha had in common.

A number of neighbours had come over to meet and greet them, many of whom had brought food as a welcome gift. Radha ran outside, still in her pajamas to find her father discussing the bill with the 'Movers and Packers' people.

Immediately she looked towards the garage and saw that the garage door was unlocked and wide open as though people had started using it. "Baba" she shouted excitedly. "Can I go and explore the garage please". "Yes, I don't see why not, but be careful" her father said. She ran towards

the open shed and her eyes started darting all around. "Oh no!" she said disappointedly as all she could find were some broken toys, rusty old garden tools and a tattered sofa set.

She was just about to turn around, where in the corner her eye caught something standing covered in a dirty white sheet. Slowly she walked towards it and pulled the sheet off. And there appeared a bicycle. Even though it was covered in dust and cobwebs, Radha could see it was the most beautiful cycle she had ever seen. And the best part was that it was exactly for her age!!

"WOW" she whispered. "This is so beautiful !!". Radha ran back into the house and grabbed a bucket and cloth to clean her newly discovered treasure. After half an hour of scrubbing and rubbing Radha stood back to admire her handiwork. And what she saw made her very very very happy!!

A cycle with all the colours of a rainbow adorned with silver bells. Golden and pink tassels hung off the handlebars, which gleamed under the light, and a brown wicker basket with bows tied on either side.

Excitedly Radha took the cycle out of the shed and showed it to her father. "Baba, I found it and I cleaned it. Finders' keepers right" "So may I please have it, please please please." Radha implored with all her might. "Yes, of course", her father replied and laughed at her excitement. "If no one else comes to claim it, you can have it for sure". That was enough to make the little girl happy.

She hopped onto her new cycle and cycled around the lawn for a while, spent her day showing off her new ride to her mother and Dadi, made friends with Savita Didi, who did not remember seeing the cycle before. And then when it grew dark Radha kept it back in the shed. "Goodnight, Rainbow cycle I Love you" we will go on many many adventures together". Radha turned and skipped back inside the house. What she didn't see was that the front light on the cycle blinked on and off. It was the most wondrous thing. The cycle had winked for sure, and then stood absolutely still.

Chapter 2

A New Friend

The next morning Radha woke up all misty eyed and sleepy. For a moment she did not know where she was. It was a new room full of new sounds. All of a sudden, it all back came to her. "I am in our new house in Kamalapur!! And I found a new cycle!!"

Radha jumped out of bed and immediately got ready. She ran to her mother, who was making breakfast. Dadi was sitting in her chair, sipping tea, pretending to read the newspaper, though in all honesty she was admiring her darling little grand-daughter and her antics. Radha leaped into her grandmother's lap and planted a kiss on her cheek.

"Good morning, Dadi, I am going out to play", she said in a chirpy sing-a-long kind of way. "Wait right there *Gudiya*," her mother said. "Have your breakfast and then you can go wherever you want." While Radha gulped down her *aloo paratha* and milk she chatted with her grandmother, "*Dadi* have you seen my new cycle?" Come with me we'll explore the mango orchard behind the house."

Radha kept on pleading with *Dadi*, but alas her ageing bones did not allow her to participate in Radha's games very often. But she did enjoy hearing about her adventures and would tell her some of her own childhood. Radha loved listening to her grandmother's stories and wished she had friends just like *Dadi* had.

Anyway, Radha chowed down her breakfast and was out of the house in no time. She cycled in the garden, around the guava tree, chatting with *maali kaka* and the parrots, whom she rightfully named *mitthu* and *pikku*, while she cycled around the house.

Soon, she was cycling in the open fields behind their house. It was a beautiful place with a mango orchard. Kamalapur was known all around the state for its scrumptious mangoes, and the township had quite a few of them. The one behind the Narain's house was flanked by mango trees on both sides and the sun rays were gliding through. It was a perfect place for bicycle riding and seemed very safe too. Radha started cycling in the orchard around the trees and on the plain ground between the trees.

After travelling a few meters, Radha found she was not alone. She saw a boy, nearly her age, with splatters of wet mud and leaves on his forehead and his shirt, with his cycle stuck in the mud. He had a huge frown on his face and was looking very worried. The boy was trying his best to push his cycle out of the mud but had no luck.

"Hello. Can I help you?" asked Radha, quite concerned. "Oh yes please, that is so kind of you" said the muddy boy with a toothy grin. So, Radha, being an extremely helpful child, got off her cycle and parked it right there. She held the other cycle from its handle and pulled with all her might, while the boy pushed at the other end. There was a whole lot of pulling and pushing and a lot of grunting and heaving, but the cycle didn't budge an inch!

The children grew weary, and the little boy was extremely disappointed. Almost teary eyed he said with a sob, "My

grandmother had sent me to get mangoes for lunch, and now I am late. The cycle belongs to my elder brother, and now it is stuck in mud and is dirty. I am also covered in mud, and now mother will give me a nice whacking for sure. I am in deep trouble", he lamented.

Both the kids sat down tired and bothered, not knowing what to do next. "I wish I could help this poor little boy" sighed Radha. Her mind was full of these little wishes when all of a sudden, she heard a squeak come from her rainbow cycle. She looked and didn't see anyone. "Must have been a squirrel", she thought and went back to being in a thoughtful mood. She heard the squeak again, and this time she went to inspect her cycle. And lo and behold what did she find???? There was a rope with a hook tied to the cycle's carrier. "I didn't see this yesterday", she muttered to herself. "Maybe I must have overlooked in all my excitement."

Suddenly as if a light switched on in her brain. She jumped off the ground, and exclaimed, "I've got a brilliant idea. Let's add some more force and pull the cycle" she told the boy. Hurriedly she took the hook of the rope from her cycle and hooked it onto the handle of the boy's cycle. Radha hopped onto her rainbow cycle and wished as deep as wishes could go:

"Please help and pull this cycle out,

let's give it all our might,

please cycle help me out,

come on let's get this right".

She gathered all her strength and started pedaling. After a few minutes, the cycle started to budge. Radha gave the pedals one last push, and lo and behold, the rainbow cycle pulled the other cycle out of the mud. "Hurray!" yelled the boy. It was quite a sight.

A beautiful mango orchard, with the sunlight gliding through with two muddy children jumping up and down with glee. "Oh, I can't thank you enough," said the boy. "By the way my name is Mohan Kumar" "I am Radha. We are new to this town." Radha happily replied as they shook hands. "My father recently started his new work here and I shall be starting school from next week too. I think it is called *Sarvodaya Secondary School*". "Nice, I study there too" piped in Mohan. "I shall introduce you to all my friends and then all of us can go cycling together." "Also, I live in the next lane. Do come someday. I must be on my way now. Thank you for all your help. I would love to stay and play but I need to rush back home". See you later Radha", said Mohan rather quickly.

They shook hands and thus began a beautiful friendship. With promises of meeting the next day, the two children got on their own cycles, and pedaled back to their respective homes. It was nearly lunchtime and Radha was both hungry and tired and, not to forget, extremely dirty. She took her cycle into the garage and covered it with the sheet. "What a day "she said to herself. As she skipped into her house, she couldn't help but wonder. "I didn't put the rope there and there wasn't any earlier either. It was definitely not there when I left home in the morning. I wonder, how it got on the back of my cycle."

Lost in these thoughts, she found her grandmother sitting in the living room knitting a new sweater for Radha. "Dadi", she shouted with glee and jumped into her lap. "You won't believe the day I have had" I met this boy Mohan who lives nearby, and we became friends instantly. There are so many mango trees in the orchard, and they are so beautiful. I had so much fun, and Mohan also goes to my new school and has promised to introduce me to his friends once I start."

She went on talking and chattering about her day and all her excitement was clear. Dadi enjoyed listening to her little one talk like this. In no time, Radha forgot about the rope and the hook which had so magically appeared on her little rainbow cycle and went on with her day.

Chapter 3

A Sunny Picnic, A Rainy Adventure, and a little bit of Magic

Time flew by fast in this quaint little town. It had been a month since Radha and her family had moved to Kamalapur, and life had started with its normal routine. Mr Narain had started work, Radha had started school, and Mrs Narain was busy with her work. It seemed as if they had lived here for years. Everyone knew and liked the new magistrate *Sahib* and his family. Very soon the Narains had become an important part of the Kamalapur family.

As Mohan had promised, he introduced Radha to all his friends; Devangi, Ria, Darsh and Myra, and soon all 6 of them became the closest of friends. Life had become very busy for even little miss Radha. The days would usually start with school, work, play and a bit of study. She hardly got time to roam around the town. But come the weekends, then she would be nowhere to be seen. Radha and her group would take their cycles and explore the entire neighbourhood. Most of the townsfolk knew each other and the children too.

On some days the six friends would cycle to a very special picnic spot. It was like their little hideaway place where they had built their own little world and would play games and eat their little snacks. This special place was situated on the other bank of a stream which had to be crossed to reach the other side. Normally the stream would be so shallow, one could waddle through it. On the bank of the other side, there was an opening of land with trees here and there. During summers it was cool and pleasant, and during winters it provided sunlight and warmth.

On a bright sunny Saturday afternoon in the month of April, the sun was shining, the birds were gloriously chirping, and the flowers were in full bloom. A perfect day for a picnic.

So off went the 6 children; Mohan, Devangi, Ria, Darsh, Myra & Radha, with their picnic baskets stuffed with all kinds of goodies and games. Between the 6 of them there were 6 bicycles. It was a jolly sight to see; their group cycling under the sun, their laughter ringing through the air. Soon they reached the bubbly brook, where they got off and waddled right across with their cycles. On reaching the clearing, they parked their cycles under a tree near their perfect picnic spot.

"Let's park right here" said Darsh who could not wait to start playing. The children got off their rides and spread the picnic blanket. Then they put all their goodies on it. Out came a football, a few dolls, who were of course joining the picnic and tea-party, and a skipping rope. The children started playing together and forgot everything else around them. Ria and Radha were on either side of the skipping rope, while Myra and the boys were jumping over it, and then they took turns. After a while they all teamed up to play a little football.

Soon enough, the children grew tired. "I'm famished" said Mohan, rubbing his tummy. "So are we" piped in the girls. So, they walked up to the stream and dipped their dirty little hands in it and cleaned their hands in the cool flowing water. Then they all sat in a circle and opened their boxes of food and placed them in the center. It was a wonderful sight to behold, a feast fit for a king.

While they were halfway through their food, down fell a few drops of rain from the sky. "Oh no!! It's starting to rain" squealed Devangi. "Hurry, let's get back home!!" By the time they rushed up and grabbed their things, packed their baskets, it was as if a cloud had burst open right over them, and it started pouring cats and dogs!

The children had no option but to stand under a huge tree. "Let's wait for it to stop" said Radha, "Then maybe we can easily go home without getting drenched". They all agreed and waited for half an hour, but by then it was still raining heavily. "Mummy will be very worried; we should go home." said sensible Myra. "It's just a bit of rain. Once we reach home we can dry up and drink some warm milk".

That seemed so comforting at that moment. All the children agreed to stick to the plan. So, they got on their cycles and rode towards the bank. To their dismay, they found the level of the stream had risen a bit due to the heavy downpour. It was no longer a short shallow brook. There was water till their waists. It seemed very dangerous to cross on foot and that too with their cycles.

Myra started crying. "How are we going to get home now? We'll be stranded here forever" The kids couldn't see any way across. The rain had become lighter, but it was also growing dark, and the children were growing afraid. Then Radha got down and whispered to her rainbow cycle.

"It's raining very heavily,

And there is no help around,

Oh! how do we little kids

Get home safe and sound?"

"Please help us rainbow cycle, please." she pleaded. Then it happened like magic. The cycle turned its tire in a horizontal position and started getting inflated on its own. From the carrier of the cycle, out emerged a foldable inflated raft. The rainbow cycle had become like a small boat to take the kids across. All the 5 children had their mouths open in disbelief.

"What is this, Radha??" cried Mohan in absolute wonderment. "Is this some kind of magic?" "I am not exactly sure what it is, but this much I know, whenever I have been stuck in a problem, my cycle has helped me out. I found it when we moved into the house. I think it is magical. It seems to understand everything I say." Replied Radha quite earnestly "But you can't tell anyone, this has to be our secret, otherwise we'll lose the cycle."

The 5 children though still amazed they all believed Radha and made a pact to never reveal the secret, and then all the children climbed onto the raft. They had also gathered some sticks to act as oars. They left the other cycles on the bank they were playing in, chained them to a tree, planning to come the next day with their parents and collect them.

Once they reached land, they all jumped out and stared at the cycle at amazement, as it turned back into a simple ordinary cycle. On their way back home, Radha told them more about magic of the cycle and they all listened in awe.

It was evening and all the kids reached home safe and sound, yes, a little wet, but safe, each with a promise of keeping the cycle's magic a secret. They were the best of friends, and between friends a promise is a promise forever.

Unfortunately, they didn't know that Amit, the local school bully, saw the cycle transform from a raft back into a cycle from his house and figured out the secret of Radha's lovely cycle. And what happened next is a lesson for one and all.

Chapter 4

There's Magic in a Good Deed

A few days had passed since the picnic incident, and Radha's friends knew about her shiny, magical, rainbow cycle, which had become the hero of the day. What they didn't know was that Amit had spied on them while they returned on that rainy day and knew that the cycle had something magical about it. There was one more thing that no one knew about the cycle, not even Radha, and that was that the cycle only came to the rescue of those who either truly needed help or needed it to help others. After seeing this magic, Amit had started to devise a mean plan. He cooked up a wicked idea where he would use Radha's cycle to help him get away after his wrongdoing. "But why would anyone give their cycle to me?" he wondered. "No one will believe me. Unless I prove to them that I am a nice person, and I can be their friend."

From the very next day in school, to the surprise of many, Amit, who was known for his rude and bullying behavior, had suddenly become kind and friendly. Little did they know that he was deceiving them. He tried helping people out in school and slowly people started to think he had changed. But had he really??

A few days later, he showed up at Radha's door looking worried and frantic. "What happened?" asked Radha bewildered "Why are you crying Amit?". "I had to go to the market to buy medicines for my sick grandfather. I ran over some nails and both tires of my cycle burst. Now I have no way to buy medicines for Dadu"!! he started howling. "Please lend me your cycle. I'll return it by evening, I promise."

Radha, being new to the place, was unaware of Amit's reputation and she agreed to help him. But little did she know that the truth was far from what it seemed. "Sure", she said "but please bring it back by evening".

"I will, I promise" said Amit, drying his crocodile tears. Radha took him to the shed and gave her cycle to him. Amit excitedly hopped onto it and started cycling away, smiling, and thinking all the while "yes, I have tricked Radha into giving me her magical cycle. Now all I need is to go into Ram Lal's mango orchard and steal all the mangoes that I can fit into my bag. I will sell them and become rich. Then all the kids will have to do as I say and treat me like their king".

With such thoughts in mind, he rode to the mango orchard, a few lanes away from Radha's house. That mango orchard belonged to old Mr. Ram Lal, who lived alone and survived on the money he got by selling mangoes from his trees.

He was a lonely old man and had no wife and no children. It was afternoon when Amit reached, and Mr. Ram Lal was taking a nap. It was the perfect time for Amit to sneak into his orchard, where he parked the cycle behind a big mango tree, which was heavily laden with juicy ripe mangoes.

"Rainbow cycle" Amit whispered, "please lift me to the nearest branch". And then he sat on the seat. But the cycle stood still. Amit repeated himself "cycle, I think you didn't hear me. I command you to lift me to the nearest branch" he said in a stern voice. The cycle still didn't respond. This time Amit was furious and kicked the cycle. This time to his surprise the seat started moving upwards. He jumped on the seat, and soon reached the middle branch of the tree.

He was overjoyed that his plan was going along as he planned. Amit jumped from the seat of the cycle to the branch and started plucking the mangoes and putting them into his bag. He was so engrossed in stealing the mangoes and daydreaming about his future, that he did not notice the seat go back down to its normal height, leaving him stuck in the tree.

And then, out of nowhere, the bell on the cycle started ringing as loudly as possible. In fact, it was so loud, that Mr. Ram Lal woke up suddenly and ran to his orchard to see what the commotion was about. He saw the cycle and a very frightened Amit stuck in the tree, unable to climb down. "Thief, Thief," shouted Ram Lal at the top of his voice, standing at the base of the tree. "Ha, you are little snively thief. How dare you steal from me. Let's take you to the police station and call your parents! I will make an example out of you, and the whole of Kamalapur will see what happens to such young thieves."

"Thief oh you little monster,

I finally have you caught,

I'll make sure you get punished much,

And learn the lesson you sought!"

He was so busy being furious and calling the police, that he didn't notice the cycle quietly moving out of the orchard on its own, and cycling itself back to Radha's shed. Mr Ram Lal went back inside his house and called Amit's parents who were of course very apologetic, and they persuaded him not to call the police.

Amit, in the meanwhile, was sitting on the branch, sobbing, and howling, begging for forgiveness. His parents were shocked and ashamed and came to Mr Ram Lal's orchard as soon as possible. Seeing their son stuck in the tree, Amit's mother started pleading and they promised, and so did Amit, that this was his last bad deed. They pleaded with Mr Ram Lal not to ruin his entire life, by involving the police. Mr Ram Lal was a very kind old man. He gave Amit one last chance and let him go. But his punishment was to help Mr. Ram Lal every evening in plucking the mangoes, to which everyone agreed.

By evening, Amit was down the tree, back home and everyone knew about his wrongdoing. The news reached the Narain house too and everyone was shocked. However, the entire truth was known only by Radha, that he had tricked her into using her cycle for his bad deed and she was very disappointed. The next day, she went to his house to scold him and tell him that she would never speak to him again. But when she reached it, she found Amit hanging his head in shame. Nobody was speaking to him, not even his favorite Nani-ma. All her anger vanished, and she felt only pity for him.

"Everyone must have scolded him by now. If I don't try to help him change then no one will." With such thoughts in mind Radha was determined to help him become a nicer person. "Amit, I hope you have learnt your lesson. It seems you know the secret of the cycle too. What you don't know is that the cycle will never help those who want to use it for their own selfish needs and greedy desires. It only helps those who want to help others. Those who are kind and unselfish", said Radha softly.

"I am very deeply sorry Radha; I lied and tricked you. I promise to turn over a new leaf. I hope people give me a chance," said Amit sheepishly. To this Radha replied, "Oh Amit, don't worry. Just be good and honest and you'll be surprised at how forgiving people can be". And then to Amit's surprise, she extended a hand of friendship.

Chapter 5

A Little Bravery & A Little Magic Saved the Day

Life went on in its usual way in Kamalapur. The children continued with their games and daily adventures, and the elders were busy with their work. The elders of the township used to finish their morning chores, and would sit in their verandahs, some reading some kitting, and some just peeling and cutting raw mangoes to make "*aam ka achaar*". And when the children used to cross their houses on their way to school, they used to greet them and sometimes, if they had time, would stop by for a sweet. This kept the elders very happy and gave them something to look forward to. Being a small town, everyone took care of each other and were always ready to extend a helping hand.

One day, while the Narain family was sitting at the table enjoying their morning *chai* and rusk, Mr Narain received a letter. He opened it and read it. It was quite clear to everyone that whatever was written in the letter made him extremely happy.

"What happened Baba? Who has written to you?" asked Radha inquisitively. Mr Narain was too engrossed and didn't listen to his daughter's question. "Tell us Beta" asked Dadi too, "who is the letter from?" "Sorry Amma, I was too busy reading the letter." Replied Mr Narain to his mother. "Actually, I have been invited to Kolkata for a seminar where I am to be the guest lecturer." It's a very good opportunity for me. I'll be gone for only one night and two days. I have to leave on the 16th and shall return on the 17th night" But I'll only go if its ok with you *Amma*." "Don't you worry about me son. I am fit as a fiddle and can take care of myself. In fact, you should take Radha's mother with you too. While you attend the seminar, she can visit her relatives who live there." Radha's Dadi suggested. "Seems like a good idea, but we can't leave you alone here" said Mr and Mrs Narain together, exchanging looks of worry. "Dadi won't be alone Baba. I don't want to go. I want to stay here with Dadi, and I will take care of her," said Radha, like a responsible adult "And it's only a matter of two days". Even the house-help assured them "Saheb, you go without any worry. We are here to take care of everything." Well, they were all happy and the trip was planned.

The day came and Mr and Mrs Narain left for the railway station. Kolkata was only four hours away by train, but to reach the seminar on time they had to leave Kamalapur before the break of dawn. Their driver dropped them at the railway station and then returned. The day went on as usual. Dadi was busy instructing Savita Didi to clean the house and cook food. However, in the afternoon, Savita received a call which made her worried. "Dadi ji, my daughter has fallen ill, and my husband is not here. Can I take the evening off to take care of her? I'll cook food for you and Radha baby and leave early"? asked Savita Didi.

"Of course, why not, you also need to have some rest" replied Dadi. "Take the evening off. Just put the food in the kitchen and I will heat it up before dinner time. Radha and I can manage for the night. But be sure to come early in the morning" replied Dadi. In the afternoon Radha returned from school and did not go out to play. She wanted to spend her time playing with Dadi. She was skipping around the house singing:

"Dadi, Dadi it's time to play,

We'll plant some flowers and dance and sway.

Dadi, Dadi lets have some fun,

We'll only rest when the sun is gone."

Out came Ludo and Uno. After playing for a couple of hours, Dadi grew tired. It was already evening. The sun had set, and Savita Didi had left. Radha and her grandmother were sitting on the verandah enjoying the twilight. "This is the best time of the day," thought Radha. The cool evening breeze accompanied by the melodious chirping of crickets. The birds had all flown to their nests. People in Kamalapur had returned to their own homes. The streets were quiet, and the streetlamps were glowing. It all gave a very serene look.

Radha was enjoying the evening while she was finishing her homework and Dadi was knitting a red sweater for Radha humming a very old song, which Radha had grown to love. She knew her *Dadaji* used to sing it to her Dadi, hence explaining her Dadi's love for that particular song. All of

a sudden there was a power cut, and the entire town was plunged into darkness. "Dadi!" exclaimed Radha. "Where are you? I can't see you".

Fumbling in the dark, Dadi held Radha's hand and tried to comfort her. "don't worry dear. We'll light some candles" and will manage for a while "first let's go inside", said Dadi trying to comfort Radha. "Come child, hold my hand and let's take the candles out of the kitchen cupboard". With the torch in one hand, both Radha and Dadi walked carefully and slowly in the dark towards the kitchen cupboard and opened it. Alas, the candles were on the top-most shelf and Dadi was not able to reach them.

By now their eyes had adjusted to the dark and it was easier to find their way around the house. "Radha beta, please get me the stool kept in the corner" Radha went and got the stool and placed it in front of the cupboard. "Here it is Dadi". "Radha I'll climb on it you just hold it carefully please," said her grandmother. So, Dadi slowly but steadily climbed on the stool and tried reaching on her tiptoes. But alas, she wasn't quite able to reach the candles, and in her effort the stool tilted a bit and Wham! Dadi fell to the ground. "Oh My God! Dadi, are you ok?" screamed Radha. She immediately helped her Dadi sit up. "Ooo" groaned Dadi. "I think I have twisted my ankle. I can't stand up. Radha, can you help me get up please. I need to sit on a chair."

Radha bent down and tried lifting Dadi into a chair. She was heavy for the little girl. But both grandmother and granddaughter were strong willed. Somehow with a lot of extra effort Radha was able to help her Dadi get up. With Radha supporting her she was able to pull herself up on a chair. "Dadi, your ankle is swollen and is turning blue. We need to call the doctor," said Radha while she gave her grandmother a glass of water. "You are right beta, but how do we do that. The phones are not working and neither guard Shyamlal nor Savita are here to help us." "What should we do now?" thought the little girl. "How do I call the doctor?"

She first gave Dadi some ice to put on her swollen ankle which had swollen badly. She remembered her mother kept some magic medicine called 'arnica' she used to apply to her whenever Radha got hurt. After rubbing a bit of arnica on her Dadi's ankle Radha sat down in the lantern and wrote a little note to the local doctor, Dr Mathur. "Dear Dr Uncle. I am Radha living at 412 Chaurasia Lane. My Dadi fell and twisted her ankle, and my parents are out of town. We do not have any help in the house. I need you to come and help us please." After writing the note, Radha folded it and put it in the basket of her cycle. "Dear cycle," she whispered, "I need you to go to Dr Mathur's home and get his attention as soon as possible. Please go as fast as you can and bring him back."

As soon as Radha went back into the house, the cycle started pedaling itself and in the darkness of the town, it was able to reach the doctor's house without being noticed by anyone. After reaching his gate, the cycle bell started ringing on its own as loudly as possible. It created quite a ruckus.

Hearing the loud ringing sounds, an annoyed Dr Mathur ran out, shouting "Who is there? Who is making such horrible noise? Come out and show your face" After looking everywhere around him, the doctor couldn't see anyone, but only a child's cycle. Maybe some child left it here, he said, as he walked towards it. "What is in here" he thought to himself after finding the note in the basket. He stood there and read the note. "Oh no, Mr Narain's mother has hurt herself, and I must go and tend to her immediately." He ran back into the house and gathered his doctor's briefcase and some bandages and medicines. Baffled as to how the cycle was outside his house, the doctor didn't waste much time. "Listen Sushma" he called out to his wife. "I am going to the magistrate's house; it seems his mother has fallen and hurt herself." Saying this, he grabbed his torch and his doctor's bag, and hurried out of the house in his old Fiat car.

He drove in such a hurry he didn't see the cycle was riding all by itself back home behind him. As soon as he reached Radha's house, he ran in to see his patient. He found her sitting in a chair, pale with pain and Radha trying to put an ice pack on her ankle. "It's ok Radha I am here now. You have been a brave and very smart girl. I am very impressed with your presence of mind".

He examined Dadi's foot and other joints. After being satisfied with his examination, he tied a crepe bandage to her ankle and helped her to her room. "Dr Uncle," said a frightened Radha. "Will Dadi be fine?" "Don't worry child, thanks to God, it is just a twisted ankle and will heal itself". "Amma just remember not to walk around too much on it". He then took out his phone and called Savita and the guard and asked them to come home as soon as possible. "Radha beta, I didn't understand, how did you leave a note with your cycle and run back home so quickly?"

Radha didn't know what to say, as she didn't like lying but she couldn't tell him the truth. "Actually uncle, I called my friend and asked him to go to you. But he is so scared of doctors and needles, that he rang the bell loudly and left the note there. After that he must have gone back to his own home. I will remember to thank him tomorrow." "Aah, now that makes sense," said the doctor. "And here I was imagining that the cycle was moving on its own".

"See now Savita Didi and Ramlal are here. I will take your leave now. Amma do take care. I will check on you tomorrow morning. It should be fine by then. After dinner take some medicine, and you will sleep fine. Namaste." The doctor then took their leave. Dadi was also feeling better. "Savita, please heat up the food for us. We didn't get around to dinner and Radha must be famished"

Radha quickly nodded in agreement "yes Didi, please give me some food fast, otherwise I'll eat an entire horse" quipped the little one and everyone in the house broke into a roar of laughter. Even Dadi laughed a lot and all of a sudden, the electricity returned, and everyone heaved a sigh of relief. "I don't like it in the dark Dadi," said Radha. "I agree Radha baby. It has been a very difficult night for you.

But one thing I don't understand, how did you send a message to Dr Saheb?" Wondered Dadi. "Oh! I had some outside help, Dadi. Don't you worry about it. All is well that ends well, isn't it." Replied Radha and then she gave a big loud yawn. "We must all go to bed now," said Dadi. "Radha you will sleep with me. Savita you will also sleep in the same room in case I need anything at night." Soon everything was tidied up in the Narain's house and the lights were out. Everything was back to its normal and peaceful self once again.

Chapter 6

Kamalapur's City Thief

It was the month of July and the monsoons had just begun. The little town of Kamalapur was bright and glistening and the air smelt of wet grass. It was at this time that a crime took place in the otherwise quiet and peaceful town of Kamalapur.

It was a chilly night, and the moon was shining like a silver surface. Its face looked all radiant and smiling. The moon was overlooking little Radha's peaceful town. It was midnight and all the townsfolk were asleep. The entire town was quiet, and one could hear the chirping of crickets and an occasional bark. The moon sighed at the sight of this peaceful town and was thanking God for all the silence.

Suddenly, he saw a shadow lurking in the darkness. It was the figure of a man tiptoeing stealthily from one house to the other. And over his shoulder was a large jute sack filled with only God knows what. This put a frown on the moon's face. He was sure, that this man was up to no good.

"Brother Star Sister Star, where are you tonight,

There is a man lurking here, it doesn't seem alright.

The townspeople need to be warned against the dangers lurking,

We need a superhero, who can protect them."

The sun rose in a few hours and the quiet town started waking from their slumber. It was a beautiful morning. The sun was clear, and the air was fresh. The birds were singing and chirping gleefully. One could hear the sound of the brooms while the sanitation workers cleaned the roads; the bell of the milkman's cycle as they pedaled to supply healthy cow's milk to Kamalapur; and the early morning clang of the temple bells and conches filling the air with their sweet sound.

And amidst all this came a shrill shriek. Old Mrs Rathi, used to live with her old husband. It was just the two of them at home, as their children were settled abroad. They had but a little money and kept all their valuables at home. Old Mrs Rathi woke up early for her daily pooja to find her house all topsy-turvy. The TV was gone along with her silverware. The almirahs were flung open and all her cash was gone. The poor old couple were partially deaf and used to wear hearing aids. At night they took them off, because of which they didn't hear a sound when the robbers must have come. When her neighbours arrived to hear what all the commotion was about, they found Mrs Rathi sitting on the floor with her head between her hands.

"What will we do now?" she wailed. "All our money is gone. How will we survive, what will we eat?" Her neighbours quickly tried to console her, and everyone joined in to help her out. They cleaned and arranged the house. Everyone pooled in to help them with money and food. Mr and Mrs

Rathi were very kind and had helped everyone around them, and now when they needed help, nearly everyone they knew was more than willing. Some called the police, some made food, and everyone arranged a little fund, to help them tide over this problem.

Meanwhile, in some other parts of the town, a similar incident occurred. A newly married couple had gone to work the previous day and came back to find an empty house, stripped of its paintings, expensive cutlery, computer and nearly everything that the thief could carry. In the following week, many other houses were robbed and there was no sign of the thief. The police could not find the person responsible for all these crimes and the town people were becoming scared to even to go to bed. Soon the townsfolk called for a town meeting which was attended by the town elders, policemen and other respected members including Radha's father. In the meeting they put their minds together and thought of a plan.

Near the banks of the river Kamala, there was an ancient temple, so old that no one knew of its origins or of the people who built it. Built of red sandstone it was as large as a school assembly hall and had many idols arranged at the back of the temple. In the centre was a *Shivling* and a huge *Hanuman* statue. Years ago, a fierce storm hit Kamalapur and nearly ruined everything in its wake. The one thing that stood erect was this very temple. Though it weathered the storm, a lot of mud and dirt was found inside it. Once the storm had passed the townsfolk got together to clean up all this dirt. While cleaning they found a trapdoor right behind the Hanuman statue, which opened to a staircase which led to a basement. When people started exploring, hoping to find ancient idols made of gold and silver, all they found were old lanterns and stone utensils. This news however did not spread far, so other than the people of Kamalapur no one knew of this discovery.

Today this gave the people an opportunity. They spread a rumour that the basement below the temple was full of ancient gold and brass idols worth a fortune. The hope was that this rumour would reach the thief's ears, prompting him to steal all that gold. The men and policemen would hide and wait outside the temple hoping to catch the thief red-handed.

So, the first night passed in a rather uneventful manner. Even *Chanda mama*, was up and waiting to see the night unfold. One night passed as did the second and third. The people started becoming impatient and wondered whether the thief had left town in search for greener pastures. Even the number of people waiting outside the temple started reducing.

On the 6th night, it was Mr Narain's turn to keep a watch on the temple along with his neighbours and few policemen. Excited and full of adventure, little Ms. Radha, on the pretext of going to bed early, snuck out of her house with Mohan and Amit, each riding their own cycles and following the elders, careful not to be seen. While the elders were sitting unaware of the hiding children, who were hiding behind a huge old banyan tree. They had parked their cycles in the temple's backyard where no one could see it.

That night while the elders started a whispered discussion on recent politics, no one noticed a shadowy figure enter the temple. It was the thief they were all waiting for, but

unfortunately no one saw him creep inside. The thief who was trying to be as quiet as possible, was shifting through some old books in the temple. In the dark he did not realise that there was a stack of utensils right next to him. Unknowingly he stumbled and the entire stack of utensils came crashing down and made loud clanging sounds. Hearing the noise, the adults rushed in, and the thief, alarmed and scared of being caught, slipped out through the back of the temple. As he ran out, he noticed Radha's bright shiny cycle parked there against the wall. Seeing this opportunity, he hopped onto the cycle and started pedaling away.

Soon the thief was a couple of kms away from the temple and the elders were still looking through every nook and corner of the temple, but all in vain. They knew the thief had slipped through their fingers. Tired and disappointed they all went home, and the children rushed back too. But Radha couldn't find her cycle parked there and went home with Mohan. She was worried about her cycle and thought "I'll tell Baba everything tomorrow and we'll report it to the police". She drifted off to sleep disappointed that the thief was still free, and her beloved cycle was lost.

The very next morning Radha woke up and sheepishly walked up to her father and admitted what she and her friends had done the previous night and how sorry she was for slipping out like that, promising she would never do it again. She also told him about the lost cycle. Her mother was horrified and furious on hearing about last night's adventure and started scolding Radha for being so irresponsible. She put not only herself but others in danger too. What if they had confronted the thief and he would have hurt them!! On seeing Radha's sorry tear-filled eyes, her anger started vanishing and she stroked her daughter's head, just telling her how worried she was and how dangerous it was to wander around at night without any adult supervision. And worse was to lie to her parents about it.

Dadi was there listening to everything. Seeing how upset she was about the entire ordeal, Dadi soothed her grandchild by wiping her tears. "Come come child, we all make mistakes in our lives. The important thing is to learn from them. But your mother is right. No matter what, you should never lie to your parents. They will be there to help you in any situation, as long as you are honest." Radha stopped crying and listened to her Dadi. "I am very sorry Dadi." I won't ever disobey any elder or lie. I will try to be truthful always" she said with a few sniffs in between. Her father took her little hand in his and said "I think you have learnt your lesson. Now let's go to the police station and speak to the inspector about your lost cycle". Radha, though she felt guilty, got ready in a few minutes, and left with her father.

As soon as they reached the station, Radha squealed in delight as she saw her cycle parked outside the station, all glittering and shining in all its glory. She ran to hug it. Seeing the child so pleased the head constable who was standing outside was very surprised. "Namaste Magistrate Saheb. Does this cycle belong to your daughter?" "Ah yes, constable sir, she lost it yesterday evening, and we had come to report its theft" How did it end up here?" asked a surprised Mr Narain.

The constable then went on to tell the whole story. "Last night, while the whole town was looking for the thief near the temple, the thief rode the cycle to the police station himself with all the stolen goods. It seems he planned to leave the city with all that, but he suddenly had either a change of heart or was scared out of his wits. He kept on muttering "save me from the ghost, save me from the ghost. Cycling himself to the police station was quite silly. But who are we to complain? We caught the thief and have been able to recover all the stolen items and some cash," said the constable. "Please come in and have some tea," he invited Mr Narain inside.

As the three of them walked inside the police station, Radha and her father could hear the thief screaming "please don't let me out!! Keep me safe here. That cycle is haunted. Please don't let me out." "Poor thing has gone mad because of all that stealing" muttered the people in the police station. "This is what happens when you do bad deeds."

Soon the whole town came to know about the capture, and everybody was talking about it and rejoicing. Radha and her family were sitting at home with their neighbours discussing at what could have happened over *chai* and onion *pakodas*.

"These *pakodas* are yummy, Mrs Narain" said Mr Chattopadhyay, with his mouth full. "Maybe the thief had a change of heart." "No-no, said Mohan's grandmother. "He must have been possessed by an angel." Everyone had something or the other to say and the guessing games continued along with the constant supply of chai and *pakodas* followed by piping hot samosas and jalebis. With the sun starting to set, it was almost the perfect way to rejoice and end a good fruitful day.

While the elders were sitting and discussing the different possibilities, the truth was known only to Radha and her friends, who were sitting on the swing in the garden. She and Mohan happily chomped away at the jalebis, grinning at the wonder of the cycle. For what had taken place last night was a secret only Radha, Mohan and the thief knew for sure. As soon as he hopped onto the cycle, rode for a few kms, he felt the cycle pedaling on its own. The thief was not able to control it and it started cycling in its own direction. No matter how much he tried, the cycle rode on its own, and despite the thief's best efforts it did not stop and cycled him all the way to the police station as fast as it could, making the thief think that they cycle was really haunted.

Maybe it was, thought Radha, or maybe it was simply magical with a golden heart of its own....

Chapter 7

It's Time for a Magical Nap

School session was coming to an end. The winter vacations were just around the corner and all the children of Kamalapur were looking forward to 30 days of fun and merriment. All kids planned to picnic and bathe in the warm winter afternoons and enjoy the evenings singing songs and listening to ghost stories by the fire. More than the children, the teachers were excited, simply because during the last week of school, just before the start of the vacations, they had planned a wonderful surprise for the children.

It was 7:30 am and the school bell had rung. All the children ran towards their classes and grabbed their seats, right next to their friends. Radha, Mohan, Amit and Devangi sat in one row. Their class teacher, Mrs Sharma, came in with a beaming smile on her face. "Good morning children". "Gooooood mooooorning ma'aaaam" they all sang together. "Today I shall be handing out approval forms for your parents". "The school is planning to take you all to the Annual Kamalapur Mela, which is held in *Netaji Maidaan*. There are different rides and yummy snacks there. But I need your parents to fill in the form and give their approval. This year, we thought instead of a picnic in the zoo, we'll take you all to the fair. Your parents can drop you off at school at 11:30 am and come to the mela around 5:30 pm directly to pick you up", informed the class teacher.

This news caused a lot of excitement amongst the children. Just two more days to go and they had so much to plan. That evening, kids in every household were requesting their parents to let them go. Radha too was on her best behavior. At around 6 pm, Mr Narain came home from his office and sat down to have tea with his family. "Radha" he called. "Yes baba", said Radha as she skipped towards her father. "How was school today? Your mother is telling me you have some school trip planned". "Yes baba" she replied excitedly. "The school is taking us to the fair in Netaji Maidan on Friday, which is the last day before winter break. They just need you to sign a form. All six of us will go on cycle, since it so near. But in the evening, you will have to come and pick me up". Said Radha in one breath." Please baba, I really want to go with my friends. I won't be seeing them for the next month, as we are going to Ranchi to visit Nana-Nani." Radha's maternal grandparents lived in Ranchi, and Radha and her mother were going to visit them for three weeks. It was the first time since their move to Kamalapur that Radha would be leaving her friends and going on a leave for such a long time.

"Ok beta, let me think about it. Leave the form on my table. I will sign it and put it in your bag tonight" "Thank you baba" Radha jumped and hugged her father and went off to plan for her big day out.

The next day in school all the children were very excited. All of them had gotten approval from their parents. Thus began their planning for their big day.

Soon they day arrived and Radha, like all the other children, was awake at the break of dawn. As soon as the first bird started its morning *raag* Radha's eyes popped open. She jumped out of bed and ran into the bathroom to brush and bathe. Unlike all the other days, she did not have to be told twice to get ready quickly. In fact, Radha was awake before anyone else in the house. Once she was ready, she ran into her parents' room. "Amma, Amma wake up. We need to pack my picnic basket. And I will help."

Her mother also got up excitedly. It was the simple pleasure of seeing Radha so excited that made her day. Both mother and daughter went to the kitchen, where they found Dadi already up and cooking something for Radha. "Radha beta, I have packed some *besan* laddus for you and for friends. I made them myself. Share them with everyone." "Yes Dadi, I will."

Radha and her mother packed a variety of things, like sandwiches, juice, fruits and Dadi's laddus. "Amma, do I have to have breakfast? Can't I eat in the mela?" "Yes Radha, you must have your breakfast. It is the most important meal of the day", replied her mother. "Do you know, whatever you eat in the morning, turns into all the energy and vitamins you need for the entire day. So, it is important to eat a healthy breakfast before you start your day." Said her mother while she gave her a full glass of Horlicks and a cheese and vegetable sandwich. Radha chomped down her breakfast and soon was ready in casual clothes and food

in her bag. The fair was very close to her house and Radha and her friends were riding to the mela. Once they reached there, they gave their attendance to the teacher and entered *Netaji Maidaan*, where the fair was being held.

To their absolute joy, they found the maidan, decked in many beautiful colourful hues, with streamers, balloons, and little shops all around. There were bouncy castles and rides in the middle of *Netaji maidaan*. There were vendors with sugar candy, lollipops, ice-creams, jalebis, samosas, and everybody's favourite *golgappa*. There were 3 different types of ice cream stalls and milkshakes stalls. On one stall there was a shooting range, where you could win any toy, you wanted (only if your aim is good enough). There were also music stalls and dance floors. Very soon the fair was full of children and many teachers from the school. There were many policemen to guard all entry and exit gates, and also at the food stalls and all play areas.

It was a sight to see. The entire day was brimming with laughter and squeals and children running here and there. By lunch many parents had come to join their kids and enjoy the company of each other and an occasional snack.

Soon it was evening, and the sun started setting. The sky was slowly turning into a beautiful shade of pink and orange. Even the birds had started returning to their nests. The teachers started rounding up the children. Announcements were made for all children to gather in the middle of the field. There would be a roll call and head count. Only then would the children be released. While the roll call was going on, suddenly the teacher stopped at a name. Ishani Anand of class-2 did not reply. Even after being called out 5 times there was no response. The teachers started looking for Ishani in the crowd, but no one could find her. Soon the teachers started panicking and asked the elder children to help them find Ishani. Radha and her friends got together and decided to ride around the fair and look for her. It would be easier and would take less time. Radha like always rode her trusted cycle and whispered,

"It is the end of school days,

Lovely cycle help us in your own way

Little Ishani is lost, and we don't have a clue,

Come let's look around, hard and true."

"Dear cycle this might be our last adventure before the summer ends, so let's make it a success. Let's trace Ishani's footsteps". So, Radha rode around the big wheel and toy stalls. But she couldn't find Ishani anywhere. The next stop was the bouncy castle. After looking everywhere around, Radha gave up looking in that area and started cycling towards the next ride. But for some reason the cycle wouldn't budge. It was as if someone put super glue on its tires. No matter how hard she pedaled the cycle wouldn't move.

Radha grew weary and irritated and shouted at the cycle. "We must move quickly and look at other places. Why have you stopped now?" All of a sudden, the cycle started circling the bouncy castle, as if it were trying to say something. Radha got off and climbed onto the bouncy castle. And there in the corner she found Ishani curled up like a kitten fast asleep. She called out to everyone and went to wake the little girl up. Rubbing her eyes, Ishani woke up and said

"Is it time to go? I got so tired from jumping all day I just lay down for a minute and fell asleep".

Everyone was so relieved that no one scolded her. The teachers were just glad that she was safe and sound. And all the kids learnt a lesson, whenever you are out with friends, you have to take care of each other and always be on the look-out for one another. Never ever leave a friend or small child unattended.

That night at home around the dining table, Radha excitedly narrated the whole story to her family. Once she was done, she gave out a big yawn. "Radha beta you are very tired and must go to sleep. Tomorrow, we have to finish our packing and catch the train to Nani's house. So, finish up with your food and rush off to bed." Said her mother.

"Haan Amma, but before that can I please go and say bye to my cycle?" I won't be long, I promise. "OK" said Amma.

After dinner Radha walked into the shed where she kept her cycle. She sat down next to it and said "Oh dear friend, I am going to my Nani's house for 3 weeks and I won't come to see you every day. But don't be afraid, Baba will be there to take care of you. As soon as I return, we can go cycling again." Radha said this as she caressed the top of the handlebars and played with the tassels. "I will miss you, but I'll be back soon."

"Sweet dreams" whispered Radha. And she covered her friend with a sheet, closed the shed and skipped to her room. "Tomorrow will be another adventure" thought Radha, "a train journey and then holiday on a farm. What fun!!"

****

I will say it again, it was quite a wondrous sight. The front light of the cycle slowly went out, like a child, absolutely exhausted by the events of the day, and his eyelids slowly drooping further till they are shut. The cycle then stood still, till its best friend Radha returned and they would once again ride together.

GLOSSARY

Valley:	Low lying are between ranges of hills or mountains.
Meandering:	To follow a winding path
Brook:	Small stream
Gurgling:	To make a bubbling sound
Nestled:	To snuggle in
Tributaries:	Stream flowing into a sea
Hamlet:	Small village
Banter:	To speak in a joking or teasing way
Zeal:	Determination
Tattered:	Torn into small pieces
Handiwork:	Work done by hands
Implored:	To request humbly
Wondrous:	Amazing
Aloo paratha:	Potato stuffed flat bread
Chowed:	To eat very fast
Scrumptious:	Delicious
Heaving:	To lift with effort

Budge:	*Move*
Weary:	*Tired*
Lamented:	*To express sorrow*
Muttered:	*Mumble*
Quaint:	*Old-fashioned*
Waddle:	*Walk like a duck*
Gloriously:	*Delightfully*
Famished:	*Very hungry*
Pouring cats and dogs:	*Raining very heavily*
Drenched:	*To make something completely wet*
Dismay:	*A sad feeling after you have received an unpleasant surprise*
Inflated:	*To fill something with air*
Emerged:	*To move out of something*
Earnestly:	*In a serious manner*
Awe:	*Feeling of respect*
Deceiving:	*To make someone believe something that is not true*
Frantic:	*Done quickly but in an unorganized manner*
Bewildered:	*Confused*
Crocodile tears:	*False display of emotion*
Laden:	*Heavily loaded with something*

Overjoyed:	*Extremely happy*
Engrossed:	*Interested in something so much that you give it all your attention*
Commotion:	*Sudden noise and confused activity*
Sheepishly:	*Showing that you are embarrassed of something you have done*
Aam ka Aachar:	*Mango pickle*
Inquisitively:	*Trying to find out about what other people are doing*
Assured:	*To make someone have confidence in something*
Serene:	*Calm*
Fumbling:	*Doing something clumsily*
Ruckus:	*A lot of noise activity and argument*
Quipped:	*To make a quick and clever remark*
Lurking:	*Waiting do to something in secret, especially something bad*
Stealthily:	*Like a thief*
Slumber:	*Sleep*
Abroad:	*Another country*
Topsy-turvy:	*A condition were everything is confused*
Shivling:	*A part of Lord Shiva that is worshipped.*
Weathered:	*To reach the end of a difficult situation*

Pastures:	*Land for grazing*
Vain:	*That does not produce result (here)*
Pakodas:	*Fritters*
Raag-	*Indian classical melody*
Panicking:	*To suddenly feel frightened so that you cannot think clearly*

www.ingramcontent.com/pod-product-compliance
Lightning Source LLC
Chambersburg PA
CBHW050614160726

48003CB00003B/1182